Dillard Quarles

AMERICAN POET

As told by Billy Plant

Dillard Quarles: American Poet
Copyright © 2023 by Billy Plant III

ISBN: 978-0-9915818-6-3

All artwork and photographs by Billy Plant unless noted in credits.

All names, other than those of public figures, are the invention of the author. Any name corresponding with that of an actual person, living or dead, is purely coincidental.

www.mazedog.com

JACKSON COUNTY SENTINEL

VOL. 24. No. 33 — GAINESBORO, TENN., THURSDAY, AUG. 17, 1922 — $1.50 A YEAR

PROHIBITION OFFICERS MAKE SUCCESSFUL RAIDS

Capture Seven Men, Destroying Large Quanity of Beer.

The Federal prohibition officers were very active in their work last week in Jackson and Clay counties.

On Wednesday, D. E. Jenkins and Walter Stone, federal officers, and Sam Whitaker, posseman, made a raid on Dry Fork of Brimstone, in the eastern section of this county.

Two copper stills, 800 gallons of beer, and all the equipment that goes with wildcat stills, were destroyed. R. A. and Walter Hatcher were captured at the still, and taken to Cookeville, where they made bond for their appearance at next term of federal court.

Friday morning, W. L. Lee, D. E. Jenkins and J. C. Tyler made a raid in the famous Union Hill section of Macon County.

Three men, Esco and Tom Moore and Bedford Moss, were captured red-handed in the very act of making a big run. One copper still, with 1000 gallons of beer were destroyed. The men were taken to Cookeville Friday evening, and bound over to federal court. Two other men were taken in custody, but were later released.

Saturday morning J. C. Tyler and D. E. Jenkins, federal officers, visited a section of Clay County, 5 miles northeast of Celina. Two young men, Hunter Reecer and Lester Beson, were captured. They were preparing to make their last run, and had only 45 gallons of beer, 10 gallons singlings on hand. This, with a 30 gallon still were destroyed. The prisoners accompained officer Jenkins to Cookeville late Saturday evening, where they made bond.

Saturday, Aug. 5, D. E. Jenkins, federal officer, with two constables of Macon county, were called out to capture what was reported to be two wagon loads of whiskey en route to Ky. When the officers searched the wagons, only a small quanity was found on the wagon driven by "Uncle" Bill Hix. Hix was taken to Lafayette and given a hearing before Squ. Meader. The wagons were en route to Kentucky, where Hix's grandson, Bilbrey, was moving.

High School To Open Monday, August 21.

The central high school at Gainesboro will open Monday, Aug. 21, at 8:30 a. m., with full corps of teachers, for a term of nine months.

We are expecting a large attendance again this year. The opening day is the very best time for pupils to enter. Those wishing to make work, cannot beginnings less inations for p given on entra who for any promoted at Those in only a cannot expect not our desire any one capable grade, nor do any pupil prom capable of

It is certain injustic to the p promoted, when but it is also hur as a whole.

We earnestly insist that the parents and school authorities cooperate with us along this line. It is so much better for the child, that it knows thoroughly each and every grade. This is why so many of our young teachers fail in the examinations. It is simply a lack of thoroughness.

We will have the Teachers Training Course again this year. All Fourth year high school pupils, who take this work and receive diploma at close, will be granted on diploma, a certificate to teach one year in this county, without examination.

As to numbers, our Teacher Training class last year ranked well, compared with other schools in the state. Only ten out of a total of 40 schools with this course of work, had a larger class than ours.

As to efficiency, we expect to to make this work, better this year than it was last year.

For the benefit of the school in general, and in order that we may hold our place among the first class high schools of the state, we are greatly in need of laboratoy equipment. It will be impossible to hold our rank without it. The cost will be approximately $150.00, for both Biology and Agriculture.

We now rank "C" as a high school, with 103 other high schools of the state. There are 96 schools yet above us. With the above mentioned equipments, we would be enabled to raise the grade of our school for the coming scholastic year. We again ask the help and hearty co-operation of all patrons and friends of our school, for the coming year.

We also invite the public to be with us at the opening, next Monday.

Very Respectfully,
H. J. Cox, Prin.

Reform does not always perform. Give us action.

It is now the honk of the auto instead of the goose that foretells spring.

An Omaha taxicab company says it lost money last year. No one has found any of it.

Working out a plan for taking care of the idle poor would be a good job for the idle rich.

A Treacherous Undertow

mule Wednesday and sustained a number of broken ribs and and other injuries, which caused his death.

Funeral service was conducted by Bro. John W. Fox, and the remains interred in the Fox cemetery late Saturday afternoon.

The deceased was a son of "Uncle" John Flatt, and was 60 years old. He had been deputy sheriff and constable of his district for a number of years, and was considered a good officer. He had lived in the 12th district all his life.

He is survived by his wife and several children, and numerous relatives.

His bereaved family have the sympathy of the entire community.

Commissioner Peck Points The Dignity of Labor.

One of the many handicaps under which the south had to labor following the Civil War, was the inherited notion among a certain class that work was ignoble and was a barrier to admission to the best society. Before the Civil War the wealthier classes owned slaves, and their children were not required to do work of any kind. They were given classical education and were equipped for some one of the professions—medicine, law, or the ministry trained for a career in politics or perhaps an endeavor made to fit them for a career in business, in banking or merchandizing.

If there was a boy who did not promise of a career in some one of the professions or in banking or trade, he remained on the farm. And it was not infrequently the case that the "dunce" of the family, the one who remained on the farm, was the one who saved the day for his supposedly more brilliant brothers by his frugality and his plodding methods on the farm.

With the close of the Civil War the slave labor was lost. Fortunes were swept away by the war, and land owners found themselves in the position of having to do the work formerly done by slaves. And they were handicapped by the lack of working capital. Many of them followed their work on the farm under the protest, determining to escape from it to some other

robbed the soil of its fertility. The gulled and washed hillsides, fields grown up with weeds and bushes, dilapidated fences and buildings, a few years ago gave evidence of this lack of interest.

Children of parents having this viewpoint grew up with the belief that the farm was to be endured only until some opportunity offered to get away from it. The industrial development of the South offered many opportunities they were looking for.

But some of our native citizens because interested in better agriculture, and inaugurated soil improvemen and better live stock programs. Some farmers from the northern states, in traveling through our State, recognized the possibilities here for crop and live stock production, and some of them settled here. The object lessons from their work opened the eyes of our people to the possibilities of our soil and climate, and helped to wipe out the prejudice against manual labor. Agriculture is being looked on with more favor. Our people are coming to realise that labor is ennobling that is productive of what the people need for their sustnance.

One handicap under which the farmer has been laboring in the slump in the prices of farm products, and difficulties have been made worse by the lack of system in marketing the produce of the farm. This is one of the problems that is gradually being worked out for the benefit of the farmer and the consumer of his products. Cooperative marketing associations in many sections of other states have enabled farmers to market their products to advantage, and these associations enabled their products to be placed with the consumer at reduced price, thus benefiting both the producer and the consumer.

A farmer produced a crop of potatoes for which he received 55 cents a bushel. In several of the bags he placed notes asking the consumer to write him and let him know what price per bushel he had to pay for the potatoes. In the course of time he received a reply from one consumer telling him that he paid $2.85 per bushel. This is a wide difference in value from the producer to the consumer, and it is this difference that it is proposed to eliminated by marketing associations. This is one of the most pressing, if

Camp Girls Enjoy Outing To Boy Scout Camp.

A number of the Camp Fire Girls had a very pleasant outing Saturday.

They visited the Boy Scouts at their camping grounds at the mouth of Hamilton's Branch on Cumberland river. They carried their lunch with them, and on arrival they found that the Dixon and Alice Tarl "Lithabra.

Prices Low In 1899.

We are in receipt of a post card from J. R. Loftis, Waco, Tex., under date of Aug. 7th, which reads as follows:

Editor of the Gainesboro Paper:

"I would like to have a copy of your paper, as mother was looking over her old keep-sakes the other day and ran across one of your town papers, dated Jan. 1899. It had Quarles' add in it, selling coffee at 10c per pound; calico 3 and 4c yd; brown domestic, 3 and 4c yd; canton flannel, 5c yd; Men's heavy shoes, 90c pair; Fine shoes $1; ladies fine button shoes 75c."

A man who steals kisses never gets caught with the goods.

Work never fagged anyone out as much as worry.

The assessor knows of many men who have untold wealth.

A love that is strong enough to break bolts and bars often goes limp when it comes time to break up a little kindling wood for wifey.

A politician may deserve to go to the stake for some of the things he has done, but the unjust criticism he has born like a martyr entitles him to a seat alongside th' own.

not the most important problems that has to be solved.

The producer should get in direct touch with the consumer by as far as possible merchandizing their products through such associations. When this is done it will be a long step toward making work on the farm as remunerative as work in other businesses and in the professions. The producer ill receive the rightful share of what the consumer has to pay for his product, and will be better able to provide those conveniences for the farm home that will make life on the farm more pleasant and make us appreciate the dignity of labor. There should be nothing but pity and contempt for the snob who think his standing is affected by honest profitable labor.

DYCUS TEAM CONTINUES WINNING STREAK

Defeats Difficult In Fast Ten Inning Game.

Dycus defeated the slugging Diffeult team in a hectic ten inning game Saturday evening, Aug. 12, by a score of 13 to 12, on their own ground, which was one of the roughest the Dycus team ever played on.

The game started, as if it would be a real good one, with Draper in the box for Dycus, in Red Springs.

The young people of Whitleyville, and some from N. S., went to Red Springs on a picnic last Wednesday and reported a nice time.

Mack Smith and family spent Sunday night in Willette.

Mr. and Mrs. Harding Shoulders, of Castallian Springs, have been visiting relatives here.

Mr. and Mrs. Benton Haile, Mr. and Mrs. Bob Meadows and children and Mr. and Mrs. Harding Shoulders took dinner with J. P. Jones and wife, Sunday. Dillard Quarles is one of the best writers of poetry that we have. He wrote a beautiful poem entitled, "May's Return."

Anna Lee Smith isn't a teacher yet, she is trying to get a position.

Edith Cassetty says the roads at Celina are very rough, or they haven't any good drivers up there.

Had an interesting ball game last Friday between Teal's Chapel and N. S. Scores 15 to 7 in favor of N. S.

Bagdad also defeated Difficult in a seven inning game by a score of seven to one.

Jay Wiggins pitching for Bagdad would have shut Difficult out, but for a horrible muff of an easy pop fly.

Batteries for Difficult; Price and Brooks; Bagdad, Wiggins and Huffines. Umpire, Canter.

There wouldn't be nearly as many marriages in this old world if the courting had to be done before breakfast instead of after the young women have had a whole day in which to primp.

UNCLE SAM'S DICTIONARY

Dr. J. L. MARTIN

What does it mean to be a great artist? We glibly say it isn't about making money or receiving recognition; we insist that we write, paint, or compose music for the pleasure of the creative act. Many artists will tell you pleasure is a weak word to describe why they create. Artists often describe a drive to create. Something that must be addressed, acted upon; a force many artists feel that, if ignored, can lead to depression, or even worse, the loss of their creative spark.

But do we create our art to help ourselves understand the world around us or do we intend it to convey a message to an audience? At the end of a person's life, are they truly a great artist if their poems, paintings, or music never had an opportunity to connect with other people, either through lack of publication or being intentionally hidden away?

In today's story we travel to the not-so-distant past and discover a poet and balladeer who, had any of his work seen the light of day, might be known today in poetry anthologies, text books, even on records of the folk revival era. But he is almost forgotten, his voice remembered only as a whisper to even the oldest members of the community where he lived

His name was Dillard Quarles.

An hour and a half northeast of Nashville, Jackson County sits in the Upper Cumberland region of Tennessee. It is a land of sylvan hillsides, dark hollows, and rocky bottomland. With the Cumberland River and Cordell Hull Lake winding throughout the countryside, it is a land of quiet beauty. Despite limited economic opportunity, Jackson County has begun to attract people from Nashville and other more populated areas who are looking to slow down and get away from the noise and bustle of the city.

One of those people is Nashville songwriter and graphic artist Isaiah Cox. Four years ago, he moved into an old farm house on Keeling Branch in the northern part of the county. I visited Cox on a sunny but cool day in early April.

(Birds singing)

COX
The house had sat unlived-in for years. It wasn't quite falling down when we found it but it wasn't far from it. We had to do a lot of foundation work and square up the old chimney.

NARRATOR
It was during these renovations that Cox discovered some old items in the loft over one end of the house.

COX
The first thing I noticed is there was this old guitar and an old pancake mandolin. Of course, being a guitar player myself, I got excited about that. The guitar was an old Gibson from the 20's or early 30's and the mandolin was what they called the Army/Navy model, made for servicemen in the First World War. Both were in pretty bad shape from being in the heat and cold and dampness all those years.

NARRATOR
Along with the instruments, Cox found a trunk containing notebooks, wax records, and an old acetate reel.

COX
As much as I thought finding the guitar was cool, I was blown away when I got to reading through the journals and the handful of letters that he had left behind. The journals are full of poems and thoughts from this guy who you could tell was a real seeker trying to make sense of the world.

6

NARRATOR
What Cox had stumbled onto in his loft was a repository of writings by a man from the area named Dillard Quarles.
Willa Dean Tayes is the somewhat official Jackson County historian, and, at eighty-four, she is among the handful of people who actually knew Quarles.

TAYES
Dillard Quarles was born in Jackson County in December 1897. He grew up on Riley Creek, about three miles from here.

NARRATOR
Tayes says Quarles grew up farming the bottomland, while hunting and logging the wooded hillsides. I asked Tayes if she had any idea what sort of education Quarles had received.

TAYES
He likely wouldn't have gone to school past the eighth grade. That's about as far as the farm boys around here went with school back then.

NARRATOR
Did you ever meet Dillard Quarles or any of his family?

TAYES
I remember seeing Dillard every now and then, playing music at a dance or church. He'd come down and trade goats or pick up some tobacco slips from my daddy sometimes. He didn't have any living brothers or sisters. His parents burnt up in a house fire and he had a brother that was killed in the First World War. I believe all this happened while Dillard was in the service hisself.

NARRATOR
Through an old service record Cox found, we know that in September 1917, after America entered World War I, Quarles joined the Navy and eventually saw sea service in the Pacific, far from most naval action in that war.

After returning from the Navy Quarles began working on river boats that cruised up and down the Cumberland to towns such as Gainesboro and Celina, hauling lumber, farm goods, and passengers to Nashville and beyond.

TAYES
Those river boats ran regularly. They called them packets, not boats. They hung on here longer than other places because we've never had any railroad lines through the county.

NARRATOR
Do you know what sort of job Quarles may have done on the river-boat, or packet as you called it?

TAYES
Just routine labor I'd imagine. But I really don't know. My cousin Ernest Meadows was a third clerk and I remember him talking about receiving goods onboard. I can still remember seeing the boats a couple of times when I was little and there was a lot of activity. Men tying up ropes and moving stuff around and such.

NARRATOR
Cox pulls out a notebook.

COX
This poem is dated March 3, 1920. I think that this must have been about the time Quarles got started on the river boats. And, I'll warn you since this is the first poem of his you're gonna hear, this one may be classified as doggerel by the poetry critics.

QUARLES (v/o)

Once more to the water's edge
Across the brow, I report to the quarterdeck
Having just returned from distant lands
I'm content to be gone again.

Heaving lines and the burning smell
Of a ship about to get under way
I gladly trade the stable earth
For a deck that pitches and sways

A bird to its wing
A horse to its hoof
But man transcended his feeble steps
When he harnessed the wind
To work for him
And took to the sea in ships

NARRATOR
Interesting, not what I expected to hear in this setting. It sounds like a mix of John Mansfield and Robert Service.

COX

So you thought that too? Good. It only gets better from there, but at least with this poem we can see this guy has already been reading other poets and started to develop themes he repeats again and again.

NARRATOR

Around the same time Quarles began working on riverboats, a group of students from Vanderbilt University and some locals with a literary bent began meeting in the home of James Frank in Nashville to discuss poetry. These gatherings eventually led to the Fugitive literary magazine published from 1922-1925. Among the so-called Fugitives were John Crowe Ransom, Allen Tate, Robert Penn Warren and other influential writers and critics of mid-20th century America.

One can only speculate how Dillard Quarles, a man of little formal education became associated with this group of intellectuals but, from a writing by Allen Tate, we know that not only did Quarles attend at least one of the group's meetings, but he made quite an impression on Tate.

TATE (v/o)

The most striking of men attended tonight's gathering of the Fugitives. Tall, with deep set blue eyes. He wore the clothes of a laborer, which he is. His speech, while not vulgar, was at times coarse. But he displayed a deep appreciation of poetry, not as one who marvels at the accomplishments of the past, but rather as someone who wants to write the poetry of the future.

The poem Quarles read that night was "Singing May's Return", a poem inspired by his experiences working the land where he grew up.

QUARLES (v.o.)

Blue sky bound summer wind
Kisses the tilled soils of May
Sweet invitation.

Mule creaking rattles
Pressed tight against the harness
Of breaking new ground

TOIL

Tempered with beauty
As birdsong rides the warm breeze
Singing May's return.

NARRATOR

The theme is in keeping with the rural life of the South which the Fugitives embraced and wrote about in their own poetry. But whereas the Fugitives took a formal, Western approach to poetry, here Quarles is writing stanzas of haiku, with the exclamation TOIL thrown in to mix things up. Aside from the fact that "Singing May's Return" is drawing  on an old Eastern form, the lyricism is not dissimilar from what you might find in a poem by Wordsworth or Shelley. "The Solitary Reaper" comes to mind.

It is unclear where Quarles may have learned about haiku but it is possible he may have been exposed to this Japanese tradition while serving in the Pacific. Whatever the case, Quarles made an impression on the group that night. A few years later Allen Tate offered his definition of a Fugitive:

Tate (v/o)

"...a Fugitive was quite simply a Poet: the Wanderer...the Outcast, the man who carries the secret wisdom around the world"

NARRATOR

One can only wonder if he had Dillard Quarles in mind.

A dozen of the Fugitives morphed into another literary group known as the Southern Agrarians which espoused a return to the old antebellum way of life as a reaction to the homogenization of American life brought about by industry and modernization of media and the wide spread dissemination of information. The group supported segregation and held prejudiced views (often tinged with sentimental drivel) regarding African-Americans.* Such views conflicted with Quarles' experiences as a laborer, where he would have worked alongside African-Americans and poor whites.

We know this because of a stream-of-consciousness entry in one of Quarles notebooks.

QUARLES (v/o)

We work together bringing the humming city what it needs down broad waters from the Ohio to Tennessee fueled by the sweating black shoulders of coalmen living their back breaking life in toil and song – sweat, sweat, even in icy February but the trip must be made in this America that is coming together, growing, growing together. The Confederate sons and sons of slaves working together for money to be made and drinking together from corn liquor jars, the occasional sip – just a sip – can't take it too far and still go on loading and off-loading, tugs towing, shoulder to shoulder passing hand to hand, bags up to the brow cross the planks to the land loading unloading working together to feed the hungry cities.

NARRATOR

What stands out here, aside from the cogent social observations, is Quarles use of prosody. The reader feels a definite rhythm in this work which falls somewhere between a poem and stream-of-conscious ramble. No one knows what, if any, influences Quarles was drawing on when he wrote this celebration of the diversity of America coming together to grow a nation. Whitman comes to mind and even more so Carl Sandburg, whose free-flowing poems often celebrated the work of blue-collar laborers. Sandburg was emerging onto the national scene at the time and it is likely that Quarles would have read some of his work by this point. But where did the sense of rhythm in the piece come from? The closest I can think of would be Jack Kerouac, but he would not emerge on the national scene till nearly thirty years after this was written.

NARRATOR

Back to the present, a cool breeze blows up the hollow as Isaiah Cox, Willa Dean Tayes, and I stand outside looking at the blossoms on an old pear tree in the front yard. Cox smokes a cigarette.

COX

No telling how old this tree is. I've heard these old pear trees can live a long time. It still bears, better some years than others. I wonder if it was here when Dillard Quarles was here? Maybe he planted it.

TAYES

I've got one in my yard that was there when I was a little girl and it still makes a right smart of pears.

NARRATOR

Speaking of growing things, do either of you know if Quarles had any children?

COX

That's another interesting part of the story.

NARRATOR

We go back inside and Cox pulls an old book out of the chest. It is a medical textbook.

COX

This is a book about electromagnetic current and its uses in medicine. It was written by a doctor at Vanderbilt, they already had a medical school back then.

NARRATOR

I look at Cox puzzled, wondering where is the connection to Quarles. Cox opens the book with its brittle and browned pages.

COX

If you look through this book, you'll notice a very attractive young woman who was a medical model. And apparently, she wasn't too bashful.

NARRATOR

Cox opens the book to a page where the woman is topless, eyes gazing downward as if deep in thought.

COX

Her name is Elizabeth Cauthron. I know that because, look here –

NARRATOR

Cox opens the book to the acknowledgements page where Elizabeth Cauthron is identified as the model. Flipping to the back page he shows me an inscription in a woman's handwriting:

LIZA (v/o)
To Dillard,
So you might remember me on those lonely nights on the boat.
Love,
Liza

COX

You see, she was older than Dillard by a few years. So, this book is from 1910, she would have been about nineteen or twenty at the time. They got together sometime between 1920 and 1923 when she would have been in her early thirties and him in his twenties.

NARRATOR

So how did they meet?

COX

That I don't know. But here is a letter Liza wrote dated June 14th 1922.

LIZA (v/o)
Hello dearest Dillard. I can't help but think of you sleeping on that hot and cramped riverboat tonight. It must seem so far removed from the intimacy we shared last week when you were in the city with me. I still think of our walks around Centennial Park, standing on the steps of the old Parthenon like two lovers on honeymoon. Or were

we more like Adonis and Aphrodite? It is hard to say. We both seem to fancy ourselves two immortals trapped in the day-to-day drudgery of a wage-earning world. I hear there are plans to refurbish that old crumbling temple so that it will last for years.

I wonder about my future and wonder what you think the future will hold. I've lived a different kind of life than many girls I've known and now, at thirty-two, I sometimes wonder if I should resign myself to the life of an old spinster. But on these warm early summer evenings I can't help but feel the vivacity of youth.

After all I am still pretty. Maybe I am vain as well, but I've learned humility through my life as a single working girl. I suppose I'll never be invited for coffee at Cheekwood, but you make me feel appreciated in a way I haven't felt since my divorce. It seems our society wants to see every woman over twenty-one clinging to a man's arm in holy matrimony. If she isn't, then she obviously must be an invalid or moral degenerate. But with you Dillard, I feel like we two are just a man and woman in love, not seeking to fulfill societal expectations.

I cherish the letters and poems you've given to me. Sometimes I read your descriptions of the river and imagine I'm there too. The last little poem about the beavers and otters made me laugh.

The otter swims in playful work
The beaver disciplines
his industrious girth
The otters have fun, swim and fish
The beaver cuts and builds
As if his wish
Was to have his busy little hands
Turn to those of a furry little man.

Good night dearest Dillard and I hope that you may hold on to this letter, read it from time to time and know that I really care for you and someone is always thinking fondly of you.

Liza

NARRATOR
Sounds like she was in love with him.

COX

Yes it does. I'm guessing he liked her too. I'll show you a very pretty poem, really a little racy for the day. I suspect he may have sent it to her in a letter.

NARRATOR

Cox turns to a page in one of Quarles notebooks. The poem he shows me is written with an odd syntax and spelling, using the letter "u" for the word "you", the letter "I" for "eyes" (the kind you see through), and the letter "c" for the verb to see.

QUARLES (v/o)

I enter u thru
The u I c
In your I's
Or (finger stroll past
Nurturing breasts)
I enter u thru
The cleft of Venus
'twixt your thighs
Or down long legs
Shapely that together bring u and I
The u I love that is soft and curls
And your arm
Which holds the hand that grasps
And fingers that caress
That part of me that
Make our flesh 1
U & I
And I love u and your I's
Where I see what makes me whole
Reflected back at me

NARRATOR

I'm reminded of another World War I veteran who, in 1923, published his first collection of poems. In the book *Tulips & Chimneys*, e.e.cummings introduced his own unique style: traditionally lyrical verse accentuated with idiosyncratic punctuation and simplified spelling. Barring the unlikely event that a nearly identical lightning bolt of poetic innovation struck twice in one year, it must be presumed that a copy of Cummings book wound up in Dillard Quarles's hands shortly after publication. Little else could explain this sudden experimentation in syntax and style.

In some ways it is easy to feel that, with its over-the-top imitation of Cumming's style, this is not among Quarles better works. But when taken out of the context of Cummings, who, keep in mind was scarcely known at the time, "I enter u thru" is actually a beautiful piece of lyric poetry. Descriptions of the form of his lover's soft body and the connection he feels with her through the exploration of her body harkens back to Walt Whitman's best poems and, to my mind, there is something reminiscent to some of Shakespeare's sonnets.

COX

I would love to know Liza's reaction to this poem, assuming she ever got to read it.

NARRATOR

I bet she would have liked it, even if it made her blush a little. Do you have any other letters between them or mentions of her in any more poems?

COX

There's one more letter and we'll get to that in a minute. I did find this poem written by Dillard in December 1923 that gives us some idea of the restlessness in his heart. I suspect his and Liza's relationship may have been over at this point. He rarely used titles but this one has one. It's called "On Knocking on a Door I Closed".

QUARLES (v/o)

Tonight I knocked on a door I closed
Hoping you would be there to open it.
But, without words, you let me know
You have granted me the life I've chose.
I walked down your street holding your hand
But the kiss I imagined was December wind
And the hand I held was a beggar's plea,
My imagination holding hands with reality
I wanted to tell you how I wish I could change
To hold you again, hear you whisper my name
Tonight I tried to but you aren't aware.
When I knocked on your door
You weren't there.

NARRATOR

Wow, that is heartbreaking.

COX

It is. The worst kind of heartbreak. It's the kind you know you brung on yourself. I could write a song around that title alone.

NARRATOR

So, is this the end of the story of Dillard Quarles and Liza?

COX

No, not quite. There's a coda to this romance. You asked if Dillard ever had any kids. The answer is yes.

Narrator

With Liza?

COX

Yes. But apparently, he wasn't too interested in being a daddy. Did he get cold feet? Did he hesitate? Did he just run off? I don't know. But here is one last letter from Liza.

LIZA (v/o)

August 15, 1924

Our child, my child, was born this past June. A big happy boy who I love more than I ever knew I could love anything in this world. I named him Charles after my father. He carries my father's surname for the time being though we will both take the name of the man I am about to marry. He is a good man who runs a printing business downtown near my work. He wants a family and graciously does not hold my first born against me.

My Charles will grow up to live a happy life in a loving home. He no doubt will ask about you someday and I'm not sure what I will say when that time comes. You abandoned me during the most difficult moments of my life, when judging eyes cast glances my way. You never wanted to know the child I carried but you will inevitably be a footnote in his life.

Please make no effort to contact me again. I hope you find what you're looking for in this life. I have. If there is anything I want to thank-you for, it is for leaving when you did. So that I could come to this happy place in my life.

Liza

NARRATOR

So sometime around the fall of 1923, Liza became pregnant with Quarles' child. Sadly, about all we know of their relationship afterward is that he left and it is doubtful they ever saw one another again. A search of public records shows Liza's life was happy but bittersweet as well. She soon married Herman Carter and they had one child together. Sadly Charles, the son fathered by Quarles, died in Europe while serving in World War II. Liza would live until 1980, dying at the age of 89, according to her obituary. It is doubtful that she ever spoke of Quarles again for the rest of her long life.

Mrs. Elizabeth Carter

Funeral services for Mrs. Elizabeth (Cauthron) Carter, 89, will be held Thursday, August 7 at 10:00 a.m. at the Waggoner Funeral Home. Mrs. Carter was a resident of 3802 Whitland Ave.

A native of Dickson, Mrs. Cauthron was born to the late Gabriel and Hazel Cauthron. She married Herman Carter in 1924 and worked for many years as his secretary and business partner at Carter Printing on Union Street. She was an avid supporter of the arts, being particularly fond of poetry and classical music.

Mrs. Cauthron is preceded in death by her husband and son Charles, who died serving in World War II. She is survived by her son, George, his wife, two grandchildren and five great-grandchildren. In lieu of flowers, the family requests donations be made to the Shriner's Hospital in Lexington, Ky.

NARRATOR

We now come to another part of Dillard Quarles' artistic journey. Along with that old guitar he mentioned earlier in the story, Isaiah Cox found a few old 78 phonograph records as well.

COX

They were all in pretty bad shape, owing to being stored in that loft for so many years. No atmospheric control, it led to some warping. They are really scratched up.

NARRATOR

Cox picks up an old record with no label.

COX

This one may have been a vanity recording, never issued by any record company of the time. I suspect it may be one of a kind. But this is Dillard Quarles' voice we're about to hear.

[Record plays]:

Thrown away
Blown away
Got holes in both my shoes
Money's something I was born to lose
Working hard
Everyday
It's all that I can do
Standing on street corners singing
My last dollar blues

(Song playing)

NARRATOR

Somehow that's not what I expected.

COX

He's playing the old 1-6-2-5-1 jazz progression which was really popular at the time. But I'm hearing an intimacy in the lyric which I think

is different from other songs back then. It's not maudlin senti-
mentality or nonsense lyrics.

(Music fades out)

COX

I listen to a lot of old-time music and I've never heard this song. I sent
a digital recording to the Center for Popular Music down at MTSU
and they didn't have any record of the song. But they did have a
record in their data base that features Dillard Quarles on guitar. It's
a really beautiful recording of "Bury Me Beneath the Willow" by the
Lytle Creek String Band.

("Bury Me..." begins playing)

NARRATOR

This sounds really good. It sounds like Quarles had a knack for sur-
rounding himself with talented people.

COX

It does. This a great recording of this song. But this is the only record I
can find by this group. The only other musical endeavor I have on re-
cord was recorded years later. It is a forty-five on the Sherwood label.

NARRATOR

So, Quarles did have a release on a record label?

COX

Not really. Sherwood was what they call a song poem label. They'd
advertise in magazines looking for people to send them poems to set
to music. There's another guy from Jackson County named Cordell
Roberts that had two spoken word sides issued on Sherwood. My
dad found that record at a yard sale and brought it home to my mom-
ma because the song talks about walking to Gainesboro and that's
where she's from.

NARRATOR

Are Quarles' songs on this record any good?

COX
I'll let you be the judge. Let's take a listen.

(Scratchy record plays)
Dirty old river
So much I've wanted to do
But you kept me from it
And how I've cussed you
But the call of the river
Is a part of my soul
Now the river is calling
And I've got to go

Dirty old river
So deep and so wide
I need you to carry
Me on thru this life
As a stranger who's drifting
On down to the sea
I trust you old river
To carry me

NARRATOR
Sounds like he's really drawing on his experience working on the riverboats.

COX
It does. And I think the river is also a metaphor for whatever it was inside him that made him so restless, not able to settle down with Liza when he had the chance for that kind of life.

NARRATOR
So, Quarles never did get married?

TAYES
No, but that's not to say he was alone.

COX
Yeah, Willa Dean's about to tell you about the big scandal on Keeling Branch.

TAYES

Well, it might've ruffled some feathers at the time but I don't 'spect anybody would bat an eye at it today. But anyways, this house used to belong to Ader (Ada) Carpenter. The Carpenters all lived up and down this creek back then and they even got a little notoriety you might say for living a long time.

COX

Wasn't John the oldest man in the world when he died?

TAYES

That's what they say. He was an old man even when I was little. Well, anyways, Ader Carpenter (that was her maiden name) was widowed at a young age, back in the twenties sometime. She stayed on the creek and she had her brothers and nephews to help her run the farm.

Well, at some point Dillard Quarles get's back from his travels and ends up here living with Ader. They never did get married. I don't know whether or not they had a romantic relationship or if it was just a matter of convenience. I never heard any of the other Carpenters say anything about it. I guess Dillard just fell right in with them. By the time I was born Dillard was already living up here and farming.

NARRATOR

And you said you remember him playing music sometimes at dances?

TAYES

Yes, just a handful of times I remember it. He'd play at church and sing a gospel song or two. Nobody would sing along. We were Church of Christ and we don't use instruments in our worship service.

COX

Willa Dean you remember that gospel song we actually have a recording of? "Shine On, Walk On" he called it.

TAYES

Oh, yes, I really like that one. I remember Dillard playing it probably not long before he left. Seems like everybody else liked it too, almost too much for a church service *(laughs)*. I remember my daddy tapping his foot and that didn't happen much in church.

COX

Beside it being just a catchy song that gets up and goes, it's interesting because it shows that Dillard didn't fall into that old cliché of the artist who becomes a cynic of his religion. And really that was a trademark of poets of his generation. You know T.S. Eliot was a deeply religious man, very involved with the Anglican church.

TAYES

Well, I won't say that I ever remember Dillard being very involved with the church but he attended like the rest of us and would get up and sing sometimes. He also played at barn dances and up here at the community center. It was the grade school back then. It had a nice stage but of course it's falling down now. A boy named Malcomb Holloway would play fiddle.

NARRATOR

Do you remember what sort of reaction Quarles received when he played and sang?

TAYES

Oh, we all liked it. For one, there wasn't anybody else around here who played anything much. But you could tell he had a real talent. His singing and playing. There was an energy to it I guess you could say.

NARRATOR

Did he ever say if he was playing a song he wrote or were they all songs he'd grown up with?

TAYES

I suspect it was both. I do remember that he had one song about a girl that had died and her spirit come back to play in the woods. I thought it was the spookiest thing but also so pretty. I remember Dillard playing that song back when I was little, and him with those deep-set blue eyes. He was a good-looking, but kindly haunted-looking man. The words and him singing just really made the song seem like something from another time.

COX

And luckily, we found the words to it in one of the old notebooks. At first I thought it was a poem till Willa Dean described the song she was just telling you about.

QUARLES (v/o) singing acapella
Racie Lee would talk to strangers
As they walked through the forest
She'd sing along with the wind and birds

A part of Nature's chorus
She'd sing her part in high harmony
As the trees began to sway
Her voice was just as pretty
As wildflowers on her grave.

TAYES

I was proud you found that song. I wish I could sing the tune for you but my singing wouldn't give you much to work with. *(laughs)*

COX

What I've done is taken some of the obvious song lyrics that we didn't have recordings for and set tunes to them, trying to intuitively look at the words and see what fits based on the sort of songs we know Dillard played.

NARRATOR

There are just so many facets to this story. So, did Dillard Quarles live out his days as a farmer, playing music at dances?

COX

Yep, and wrote some pretty good poetry about it too. That would be the storybook ending wouldn't it!

NARRATOR

So how does the story end?

TAYES

We don't rightly know. I remember at some point, I guess it was in the late sixties, Dillard was just gone. Of course, I was raising my young un's by then and was too busy to worry about it much. But I remember anytime we drove by, Ader would be sitting on the porch, usually with her sister Sara at that point. We'd stop by and check in on them and they'd just be sitting there dipping their Brutons snuff. A lot of women from their generation dipped.

NARRATOR

Ada never mentioned Quarles?

TAYES

No, never said a word about him. She never talked too much anyway. Sara would talk about the weather, if it was hot or rainy, ya know, but they really just seemed to live in the moment, I guess you could say.
(Pause)
I sometimes wish I knew what they talked about amongst theirselves.

But life was really different back then in some ways. Slower and quieter. No TV, nothing beeping or ringing and carrying on like we're surrounded by now. In fact, I don't recall Ader ever had electricity in the house till the early seventies

NARRATOR

You would think Quarles would have craved that peace in his later years.

TAYES

I don't know that Dillard Quarles was ever one for settling down, even though he did stay here for thirty years or so. I imagine he just wandered off one day. Seems kindly selfish to me, to just leave Ader here alone like that once she got older.

COX

I think Dillard Quarles probably suffered from that incessant need to create that torments some artists. There's a couple of notebooks here full of poems. Some good, some are doggerel. I suspect there was more but he may have taken those with him.

TAYES

It would be interesting to know what became of him. He sounds like quite a character but nobody around here would've known it if you hadn't of found that trunk. Truth is, I'd nearly forgotten about Dillard till Isaiah asked me if I knew who he was.

COX

Yeah, it's been an interesting journey. Whether or not we ever find out where Dillard Quarles wound up, at least we have this collection of his writings that now we're sharing with the world. Who knows, he may become a celebrated poet yet.

(Music plays to seperate the scene.)

NARRATOR

So there you have it, the story of the mysterious poet and balladeer Dillard Quarles. You can find more of Dillard Quarles poetry, some accompanied by the artwork of Isaiah Cox in Cox's forthcoming book, Dillard Quarles: American Poet, to be published by Maze Dog Media later this year. To hear more of the music of Dillard Quarles you can visit Maze Dog Media dot com and click on the link: DILLARD QUARLES.

POEMS

What follows is a collection of poems recovered from Dillard Quarles notebooks. Being an artist, I could not resist the urge to offer my graphic interpretation of Dillard's work. I hope you enjoy these poems and feel a connection to the thoughts they convey and the cadence of Quarles' speech.

Sinecerely,

Isaiah Cox

There is a dimly lit place
Deep in my heart.
In that space, closed off and guarded,
I keep an eternal flame burning bright,
Bright but hidden.
A great yearning,
With hands outstretched to the sun.
An appeal that heaven may hear my
hopes,
The fates lend an ear to my desires.
That somehow the stars will align
In such a way that
My great yearning is answered
And my dreams become real
Beyond the stardust of hope,
That my words may be heard
And resonate as a true statement
Of what it means to be a person
Trying to understand this world.

All things are a continuous becoming
And who we are today is but one flap
Of a butterfly's wing
On an ephemeral journey
As if death closes the book on the
Development of our soul.
But I still try to identify who I am
With mixed success.
The hawk has his identity of feathered flight
Strong talons and keen eyesight
But my wings are more unsure.
Man's dilemma is his searching spirit:
Rather than being the essence of what he is
He further seeks to answer the question of
Who he is.
Perhaps if I could lose myself
I would find my true meaning
That has been born into me
All along.

The earth I walked was as brilliant
as the blue sky of my dreams
I felt free
and I felt connected to the universe
Beneath my feet
and within my heart
I felt like I was a river
Always there but ever changing

Stones sit heavy in this hallowed hall
My lonely moonlight cloistered walk
Where gothic spires soar like hopes
On the clock tower belfry.
I was meant for an academic life
Learning, reading the classics
Laughing at jokes in Greek
But my road never led here,
My curiosity derided, never understood
It couldn't haul a log
Off the hillside
Or hang tobacco in the barn.
Now I walk in the moonlight,
A stranger exploring a forbidden world
And I know I too can think
Of heady ways of saying simple things
In the language of affectation.
Listen to me now:

The stars that astral journeys run
Illuminate my
i-madg-in-a-shun
Till I hardly know in which world I stand
A poor roustabout or a college man.

The darkness is kind to those who dream
It allows me to walk
Through hopeless landscapes unseen.
Not for fear I'll be run away
I shed my tears
Because I can't stay.

A cloistered walk at the University of the South in Monteagle, Tenn. After serving as U.S. Poet Laureat from 1943-1944, Allen Tate became editor of the school's literary journal from 1944 thru 1946, transforming it into one of the more pretigous publications in the country, He is buried in the University Cemetery on campus.

It is a loss to literature that Dillard Quarles was never able to join the ranks of Academia. I think the poem on the facing page shows that at one point he desired that intellectual stimulation.

I.C.

We are sprung up from the place
where we were raised.
Our muscles are shaped,
our sinews toughened
by the weight of the rocks we moved
from the field;
the trees we felled
the hard pounding of nails into that
wood
to build the sheltering roof;
we are the force of the water we swam
against
to cool off on summer days
from the sun that baked our skin
and pulled the sweat from our bodies.
We are the nutrition of the beans and
corn and flesh
and we are built by what grew those
things from the earth.
The place where we grew and worked
and played
has marked our bodies.
Where I'm from the ground was rich
The water was sweet
The cooling breeze a refreshing breath;
And when, from time to time, I return to
those green hills
I can almost hear the breeze whisper
"You are home."
As the flowing creek winds its way
through the rocks of time
Singing a lullaby as I lie down to dream.

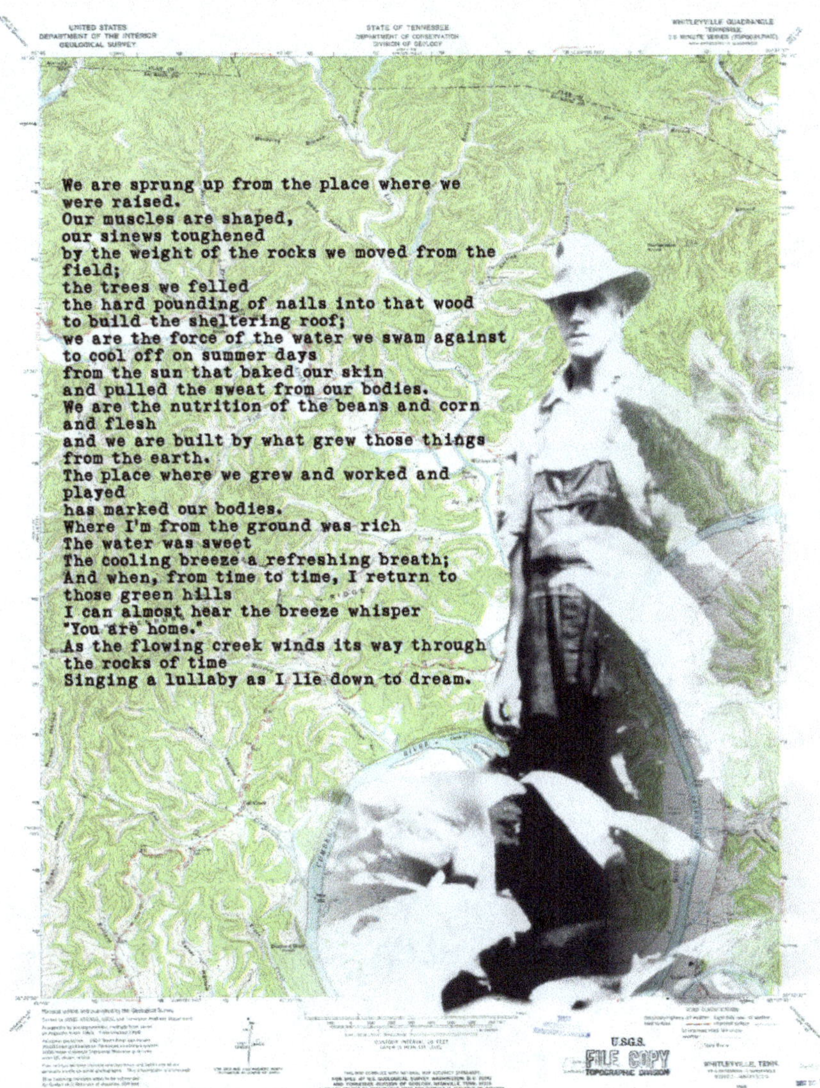

We are sprung up from the place where we
were raised.
Our muscles are shaped,
our sinews toughened
by the weight of the rocks we moved from the
field;
the trees we felled
the hard pounding of nails into that wood
to build the sheltering roof;
we are the force of the water we swam against
to cool off on summer days
from the sun that baked our skin
and pulled the sweat from our bodies.
We are the nutrition of the beans and corn
and flesh
and we are built by what grew those things
from the earth.
The place where we grew and worked and
played
has marked our bodies.
Where I'm from the ground was rich
The water was sweet
The cooling breeze a refreshing breath;
And when, from time to time, I return to
those green hills
I can almost hear the breeze whisper
"You are home."
As the flowing creek winds its way through
the rocks of time
Singing a lullaby as I lie down to dream.

35

Once more to the water's edge
Across the brow, I report to the quarter-
deck
Having just returned from distant lands
I'm content to be gone again.

Heaving lines and the burning smell
Of a ship about to get under way
I gladly trade the stable earth
For a deck that pitches and sways

A bird to its wing
A horse to its hoof
But man transcended his feeble steps
When he harnessed the wind
To work for him
And took to the sea in ships

Dillard Quarles served on the stern-wheel packet Jo
Horton Fall, *seen here on the Cumberland River.*

Blue sky bound summer wind
Kisses the tilled soils of May
Sweet invitation.

Mule creaking rattles
Pressed tight against the harness
Of breaking new ground

TOIL

Tempered with beauty
As birdsong rides the warm breeze
Singing May's return.

OTTERS & BEAVERS

The otter swims in playful work
The beaver disciplines
his industrious girth.
The otters have fun, swim and fish
The beaver cuts and builds
As if his wish
Was to have his busy little hands
Turn to those of a furry little man.

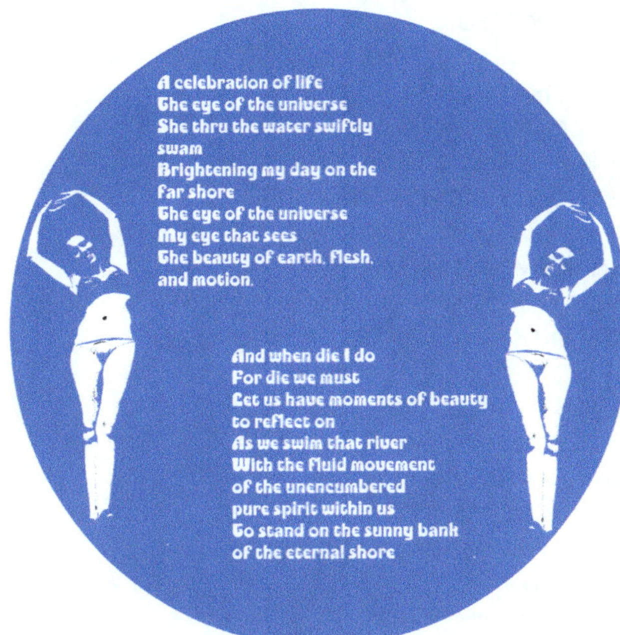

A celebration of life
The eye of the universe
She thru the water swiftly swam
Brightening my day on the far shore
The eye of the universe
My eye that sees
The beauty of earth, flesh, and motion.

And when die I do
For die we must
Let us have moments of beauty
to reflect on
As we swim that river
With the fluid movement
of the unencumbered
pure spirit within us
To stand on the sunny bank
of the eternal shore

How many times have I walked these streets,
Wishing I was not alone?
Corn liquor and a cigarette
Haunted by memories of home.
And as I get high, I feel regret.
Regret for the vagabond life I have lived.
A sailor tied to an inland sea.
Looking inward, I wonder where my ocean is,
Wandering this world alone, but free.
My learned friends have a different path,
Expressing themselves with words that pay.
But I don't want to be like them.
Their thoughts seem to be looking back
On a past from which I walk away.
New horizons will come in time
But tonight my soul sighs with care.
A little drunk, with a wandering bone,
Down by the river
Where people sit and stare.

On the shrouded mountaintop
stormy wind and clouds
Hold no fear
For a traveller
With a path to follow.

***

The heavens speak of the promise within you.
The whisper of a star
The shout of the blazing sun.
Do your work and know
The heavens speak well of you.

Two girls in a red canoe
Floating down the river wild;
Green riot of summer:
Bird screams buzzing insect wings.
They paddled up a creek
That led up the hollow
Under the shade of enclosing trees
On the dark side of a hill.
The sylvan nature they found,
Twisted sycamores and arching maples,
Cast gothic humors
Over ledges of decaying rock.
Tying their canoe to a bent sapling
They wandered up the inviting creek
(Not a welcome of warmth and peace
But like some old spirit beckoning).
They wandered till the air it seemed
Carried the tune the fairies sing
As a voice on the cool breeze
Said "Come play with us in the shade of the trees."
The girls could not turn around,
Filled with fright but adventure bound
Abandoning their careful steps
They ran forward with bounds and leaps
Till they came to a cold-water spring
Silty sand bottomed, its water glist'ning
In a stray shaft of sunlight
That shone through the leaves
Reflected off old marbles
Scattered in the sand.
Colorful marbles in such a wild place
While all 'round was quiet but
For the gurgling spring.
Suddenly both girls let out shrill screams:
While marveling marbles in the sand
It's frightening to feel
The touch of little wet hands.

I think this strange little poem presents a haunting image. I'll call the style
sylvan gothic. Dillard would tap into this mood in one of his songs as we shall
see in a few pages.

I.C.

I enter u thru
The u I c
In your I's
Or (finger stroll past
Nurturing breasts)
I enter u thru
The cleft of Venus
'twixt your thighs
Or down long legs
Shapely that together bring u and I
The u I love that is soft and curls
And your arm
Which holds the hand that grasps
And fingers that caress
That part of me that
Makes our flesh 1
U & I
And I love u and your I's
Where I see what makes me whole
Reflected back at me

I enter u thru The u In your I's Or (finger stroll past Nurturing breasts I enter u thru The cleft of Venus' twixt your thighs Or down long legs Shapely that together bring u and IThe u I love that is soft and curls And your armWhich holds the hand that grasps And fingers that caressThat part of me that Make our flesh 1U & I And I love u and your I'sWhere I see what makes me whole Reflected back at me

Tonight I knocked on a door I closed
Hoping you would be there to open it.
But, without words, you let me know
You have granted me the life I've chose.
I walked down your street holding your hand
But the kiss I imagined was December wind
And the hand I held was a beggar's plea,
My imagination holding hands with reality
I wanted to tell you how I wish I could change
To hold you again, hear you whisper my name.
Tonight I tried to but you aren't aware.
When I knocked on your door
You weren't there.

So much the less for having loved her
Such is the feeling of loneliness after good-bye
But there is a smile creeps across my face
For having known her in the first place.

A song is a memory in the city street
Thinking how once we walked thru hand in hand
Not filled with the pomp of a proper lady
Nor the fine dress of a gentleman

But just two people, younger then,
In love as we understood it at the time,
Exploring a world of sensual treats
In kisses, songs, and delicious sweets

If life is a mix of good and bad,
A scale that teeters stone by stone
With her I was happier beyond measure
Than I have ever been alone

I have heard them singing to me,
Lonely sailor out at sea.
Calling from distant rocks
Or cutting coral;
The mermaid song that tempts like fate,
A siren song. I can't turn away.
For the beauty of the voice I hear
Is the sweetest summons spoken soft
Amid the ghost whisper of ocean spray.
And the mouth must hold more beauty yet,
With lips so supple and wet,
Worn on a face with eyes that shine
That pull me toward her as if gazing into
mine.
How I imagine her breasts and thighs,
Soft curves that greater pleasures belie.
But I'm surrounded all the time by men
From bow to stern and back again.
When a man is long at sea he dreams
And in my dreams the mermaids sing.

In this poem I imagine Dillard captures a sentiment shared by many young men in the armed services back before women were allowed to serve alongside them. I can attest that a crowd of men for months on end can be a lonely place. The water the girl stands in is from a 2003 photo I took off the coast of Guam. Dillard Quarles sailed these same waters while serving in the Navy during World War I.

I.C.

I live day to day much like my neighbors,
People I have known my whole life.
They know me for who I am in working clothes under the sun,
Possibly think I am a little odd.
But they don not know my inner world.
I am nothing special, any more than we are all special.
There is no reason why other people
                              should concern themselves
With the thoughts I think when deep in thought.
Some say I am haunted by my past.
Yes, this is true.
But I am haunted as well by what is to come.
Like all people, I have a message inside me.
Will anyone listen?
Will I find the eloquence to make people
                    want to hear what I have to say?
I write it down as the notion comes over me.
I know I'm getting close to finding the words.
But still, I walk up on the ridge
And listen to the wind.
Some say this is the voice of God.
But even if He is screaming these long-sought truths to me
I can barely hear it.
But I do hear something.

                              I will continue to listen...

Old Polaroid dated 1991 taken from ridge above Jennings Creek.The Spivey house (upper right) and barn no longer standing. Keeling Branch runs along tree line just past the house. This location on the ridge was a favorite of Quarles for the wide panorama created by the bend in the large creek.

Life demands a committment to a course of action.
When the fledgling hawk first stretches his wings
He expresses faith in a promise.
His leap from the nest does not require courage
But rather confidence in the fact
That he was born to fly.

At sunset's orange horizon
I watch the geese fly their peculiar formation.
Shortening days their cue
To a changing of the season.
I think about my own migrations,
How shortening days
Call the wanderer to travel
North or south
According to his own proclivities
Of origin and birth.
A season spent where lovers meet,
But as days grow shorter
I'm drawn home again

Poetry is more interesting when there is
no muse to flatter with worn out senti-
ments.
-   No pseudo-anguished angst bleed-
ing onto the page

-   No overblown fondness for a season
forcing an outflow of florid inanities
about Spring wildflowers in bloom.
Poetry is most interesting when it states
a simple truth,
arrived at through a longing to express
a rational thought in a different way.

Of all my gushings, some of my best
poetry speaks on a blank page.

This poem reads to me
like a brief commentary
in poetic form concern-
ing the New Criticism,
of which, Quarles' old
acquaintances Allen
Tate and John Crowe
Ransom were primary
proponents. Something
in this poem reads a
little tongue-in-cheek to
me. I can even imagine
Dillard giving us a wink
as he wrote the last line.

I.C.

In the hard light of 30 years reality I find
I may not be a poet
But if not
Then what am I?
Maybe we are the echoes
Of the wind and the water
Putting the song of birds into words we
can understand

Picking up an arrowhead is like sticking your hand through a
rainbow.
A fleeting door that has opened allowing you too reach
beyond your time
To interact with others who once walked these hills.
Behold their craftsmanship, appreciate how they worked
To feed and clothe themselves.
As the winter wind blows across your face
So they felt its sharp bite on theirs
As your muscles tighten walking up the ridge;
As your lungs heave deeper for the breath to carry you on.
So too did they feel the pull of the land as they traversed the
hills and hollows
You have both called home.
And as darkness descends and you are startled by the cry of
the bobcat in the night
Perhaps they were stirred to go forth into that darkness
Moving with the creatures they depended on in their quest
for survival.
Not toiling like you in an effort to subdue the land and the
creatures upon it,
But to exert their place in the primeval order of the natural
world.

Finding an arrowhead is like sticking your hand through a
rainbow
And grasping something from another time, albeit the same
place.
A person long dead having made it
A person with no concept of your world
And you having little concept of his
Rainbows seperate great realities
A beautiful, transient curtain

Picking up an arrowhead
is like sticking your hand
thru a rainbow...

He'd play at barn dances and up here at the community
center. It was the grade school back then. It had a nice
stage but of course its falling down now...

SONGS

When I moved into the house I discovered some old records and that old tape reel in the loft. Of course, the records were warped from heat and dampness. The tape was brittle and required some serious preseravtion work before I could listen to it. Time had not been kind to these old recordings, but they still allowed me to hear Dillard performing some of his songs. From this I learned how he phrased lyrics and what sort of melodies he sang. Using these old records as a guide, I've put music to the song lyrics I found in the old notebook. There are also a few instrumentals of Quarles playing mandolin. These songs will eventually be available on an album dedicated to the songs of Dillard Quarles.

Looking Back On My Life

In the quiet of the night
I look back on my life
Like a book opened to
My favorite page
Happy mem'ries that I find
Play like pictures in my mind
And it's good to recall
Those younger day

To remember Mom and Dad
Makes me happy but a little
sad
My momma was so pretty
In every way
Daddy was a quiet man
With steady eyes and cal-
loused hands
They worked hard for eacho-
ther
Every day

Me and brother worked the
fields
With two mules and logged
the hills
And talked about
All the things we'd like to do
He'd play is fiddle tunes at
night
In the summer moonlight
I'd pick the guitar
And sing a song or two

But if a man wants to see
The world, he has to leave
And too soon I was on my
way
When I returned to my home
The old place was gone
And Death had called
My family away

I wandered lonely
as a feather
Tossed around in windy
weather
I had to move, nowhere
could I stay
A girl came into my life
We shared our dreams by
candlelight
I don't why
I ever pushed her away

Tonight I'm lost in reflection
The road that's brought me
Where I stand today
There's a girl who's name
I can't mention
Like my momma, she was
pretty
In every way

Last Dollar Blues

Thrown away
Blown away
Got holes in both my shoes
Money's something I was born to lose
Working hard everyday
It's all that I can do
Standing on street corners singing
My last dollar blue

I woke up this morning and went out to pay some debts
When I went to spend a little on me
The wasn't nothing left
So I just grabbed my old guitar it's all that I can do
Standing on street corners singing
My last dollar blues

For dollar bills that I ain't got
I slave my life away
Maybe me and this old guitar
WIll make it big someday
Until then I'll pick and grin
It's all that I can do
Singing for other working folks
About my last dollar blues

Racie Lee

Racie Lee would talk to strangers
As they walked through the forest
She'd sing along with the wind and birds
A part of Nature's chorus
She'd sing her part in high harmony
When the trees began to sway
Her voice was just as pretty
As wildflowers on her grave.

Racie Lee would whisper low
To weary travelers as they passed
They would turn in great surprise
At the cool breeze at their back
A woman child stricken down
Just as she'd come of age
Racie Lee had the world to see
Not bound by an early grave

The sun that shines so bright
Brings light and warmth to all
The breeze that blows 'cross green hillsides
And weeping waterfalls
A child of Nature found a home
In a soul that flew away
Now Racie Lee sings with the birds that fly
Not bound by an early grave.

Racie Lee would talk to strangers
As they walked through the forest
She'd sing along with the wind and birds
A part of Nature's chorus
She'd sing her part in high harmony
When the trees began to sway
Her voice was just as pretty
As wildflowers on her grave.

Dark and Stormy Night

Dark and stormy night Oh how you try my soul
How you cause me to tremble inside
Something within your dark shrouded gloom
Echoes the darkness in my mind
Sometime ago my heart went astray
Like your wind blowing wild and so cold
Now just like the leaves that you blow from the trees
Tonight I'm so hopeless and old

Dark stormy night with your wind and your rain
Your lightening and thundering air
You remind me too much of this life I have chose
Of sin and of reckless despair
Somewhere on the shores of a far distant land
The moon is shining stars are shining too
A calmness like that I will not know again
For my dreams lay all scattered and through

Dark stormy night let your wind take me too
Pick me up in your tremulous hands
Carry me away in your dark shrouded gloom
Take me to some far distant land

Don't show me heights that I never will reach
Don't do that to this troubled man
Just blow me to some fairer place where worries will cease
As if I were a leaf on your wind

Dirty Old River

Dirty old river
We're rolling again
Thought I'd stay for awhile
But heard you calling my
friend
Once in a while I stay behind
But the river keeps rolling
Rolling right thru my mind

Dirty old river
You'd think you were mine
But now I've realized
I was your all the time
Roll down to the ocean
'Cause that's where you end
And I'll be going with you
Old river my friend

Dirty old river
Banks so far apart
That no one can swim you
That's how you break hearts
You leave lovers waiting
On the far side
Then come wash away
The tears that they've cried

Dirty old river
Old and yet pure
The wisdom of ages
Washes off of your shore
Dirty old river
Keeper of time
Let me go with you
Your wisdom to find

Dirty old river
So much I've wanted to do
But you kept me from it
And how I've cussed you
But the call of the river
Is a part of my soul
Now the river is calling
And I've got to go

Dirty old river
So deep and so wide
I need you to carry
Me on thru this life
As a stranger who's drifting
On down to the sea
I trust you old river
To carry me

Pale Lover

Pale Lover
Discover
The light of the life outside
Shines down
All Around
To dry up the tears you've cried
Rivers run a sure path to the sea
Trees reach to the sky to be free

Free minds
In time
Become the light they seek
Ready hands
They can
Build trails for wandering feet
Where you go you carry where you've
been
It's part of who you are but not the end

Night stars
They are
Bright moments along the way
Sunrise
Painted skies
As light moves across the day
Envision what you want your life to be
Then look within to create what you see

Life is good.
Go for it till all you find in you is you.

I'm not sure when the hippie movement made it to Jackson County but it seems Dillard may have been a harbinger of the expanding consciousness that was sweeping across the nation in the 1960's. I felt like this poem was begging to be set to music. These words carry a vibe of coming out of darkness into a new awareness. It was my goal to write music for it that carries the same feeling. Far out man!

I.C.

When You Walk Through a Door
(for the very last time)

When you walk through a door
For the very last time
When it swings open
And no ones inside
Memories dance
In the dust on the floor
But the people you love
Don't live there no more

I went to the place where
My momma was born
The door stood wide open
The paint faded and worn
But as I crossed the threshold
Years melted away
And I heard the laughter
Of earlier days

I saw my grandma
Standing at the stove
Grandpa with his pipe
Packing a bowl
My aunt at the table
Snapping string beans
It was late summer
And they were canning every-
thing

Then my momma walked in
Through the back door
She stepped right up to me
And embraced me once more
"Momma I love you
And I miss you so.
I know that I'm dreaming
But I don't want to go."

Bridge:

Then the light
Faded out
Of the windows
And the chill
Returned
To the air
My memories
Stepped back
Into the shadows
Like voices
You hear
That aren't there

When you walk through a door
For the very last time
When it swings open
But no ones inside
Memories dance
In the dust on the floor
But the people you love
Don't live there no more

I.C.

Shelter From the Storm

When rain is falling in my soul
And the night is dark and cold
When the winds of doubt
Blow 'round the lonely flame
I take comfort because I know
There is somewhere I can go
To take shelter from the storm
That has no name

Ever since I was a child
I've roamed and wandered wild
I'm the drifter who is
Knocking at your door
You don't have to take me in
But I know you will again
Give me shelter
From the storms of life once more

You know shelter from the storm
Is nothing like a home
But I've known you for so long
That it feels right
And it seems you need me too
Waking up here next to you
To be your shelter from the storm
On lonely nights

Bridge:
The world goes round and round
Sun comes up, sun goes down
I won't call it love
What I feel
But it's enough

I'm not sure Dillard would have written this Beatles-esque melody, but he lived at a time when music was changing. He seemed to be an inveterate innovator and experimenter with his poetry and I can only imagine he would have done the same with his music.

On another note, these lyrics are from a newer looking notebook and written in an older hand than the entries about Liza. I think this song tells us as much as we'll ever know about his relationship with Ada.

I.C.

Lonely Winter's Day

Snow skies and gray
On a winter's day
No lover can be found
Beer and booze you know
I wouldn't choose
But it's the only comfort
That hangs around
I'm happy and then
It's gone again
And this dark old world
Grows darker still
When I awake
Plan my escape
But the bottle always calls
So I never will

Skeleton trees
Just like me
My heart's as empty
As the barren ground
No summer breeze
Stirs green leaves
To paint sunshine
On winter's brown
I have nothing to say
Throw it all away
Words can't find feelings
That aren't around
If she only knew
But I'm just a fool
If love won't come to you
You cant chase it down

Lonely winter's day
Feel like running away
But running away's
Not always what it seems
Its what's inside
You can't run and hide
Metal wings can't give flight
To paper dreams
I'm just a rock that skips
On the face of the ocean
If I didn't move
I'd sink right down and drown
But there's no peace for
A rolling stone
No warm bed for me
To lay my head down

Roll On Ol' River

Roll on ol' river
Let the rain fall, wind blow
Roll on ol' river
Riding on your rising flow
Carry me fast
I've got somewhere to be
Want to see my girl
Down in Nashville, Tennessee

It's been too long
Since I held her close to me
And heard her sweet voice
Just as pretty as can be
So roll on ol' river
A little faster if you please
Take me to my girl
Down in Nashville, Tennessee

Bridge:
Roll on ol' river
Past the farms and fields
Wind your way round
The bottomland and hills
Roll on past Hartsville
And wherever we may be
Take me to my girl
Down in Nashville, Tennessee

Roll on ol' river
Now we're coming round the bend
It feels so good
To see this town again
It's been too long
Since I walked those busy streets
With the girl I love
Here in Nashville, Tennessee

Cumberland River, Nashville, Tennessee. February 2009.

Shine On Shine On

As I wander through the
valley
Of the shadow of doubt
I pray that God's grace
Will help lead me out
That I may find my way
On the right road again
In the light of His blessings
And washed of my sins

Shine on, Shine on
Like a beacon above
Walk on, Walk on
In the light of His love

I carry the burdens
Of choices I've made
That I can't forget
But His Love forgave
Like a leper who wanders
Scorned by the world
That holds onto filth
But casts away pearls

Shine on, Shine on
Like a beacon above
Walk on, Walk on
In the light of His love

The eternal light
I follow today
Can still shine on you
And show you the way
If you should stumble,
Backslide, or fall
His Love holds the promise
That restores us all

Shine on, Shine on
Like a beacon above
Walk on, Walk on
In the light of His love

(Acappella)
Shine on, Shine on
Like a beacon above
Walk on, Walk on
In the light of His love

And with that, it appears that Dillard Quarles walked on.

Credits:

Elizabeth's photo:
High Frequency Electric Currents in Medecine and Dentistry. S.H. Monell, M.D., William R. Jenkins Company New York, 1910.

Newspaper on page 4:
Jackson County Sentinel. August 17, 1922. Newspapers.com
https://www.newspapers.com/image/859644488/

Geese vector for "Migration" - modified from dreamstime.com

"Born to Fly" hawk - Modified from Bing AI generator

Mermaid poem image (girl only):
"Jugend [German art magazine]" (1903).

Likeness of Dillard Quarles:
Photo of Ernest Meadows (1900-1978). Photographer unknown.

9 780099 581863